D1074664

Original Korean text by Ji-hyeon Lee
Illustrations by Bo-mi Shin

This English edition published by big & SMALL in 2016
by arrangement with Aram Publishing
English text edited by Joy Cowley

Distributed in the United States and Canada by
Lerner Publishing Group, Inc.
241 First Avenue North
Minneapolis, MN 55401 U.S.A.
www.lernerbooks.com

ISBN: 978-1-925249-00-2
Printed in Korea

We Need Soil

Written by Ji-hyeon Lee
Illustrated by Bo-mi Shin
Edited by Joy Cowley

Soil is the top layer of Earth
that covers the land.
We need soil.

We can dig in soil.
It is moist and dark.

Ants and earthworms live in soil.

Soil is home to many small animals.
Do you see their burrows and tunnels?

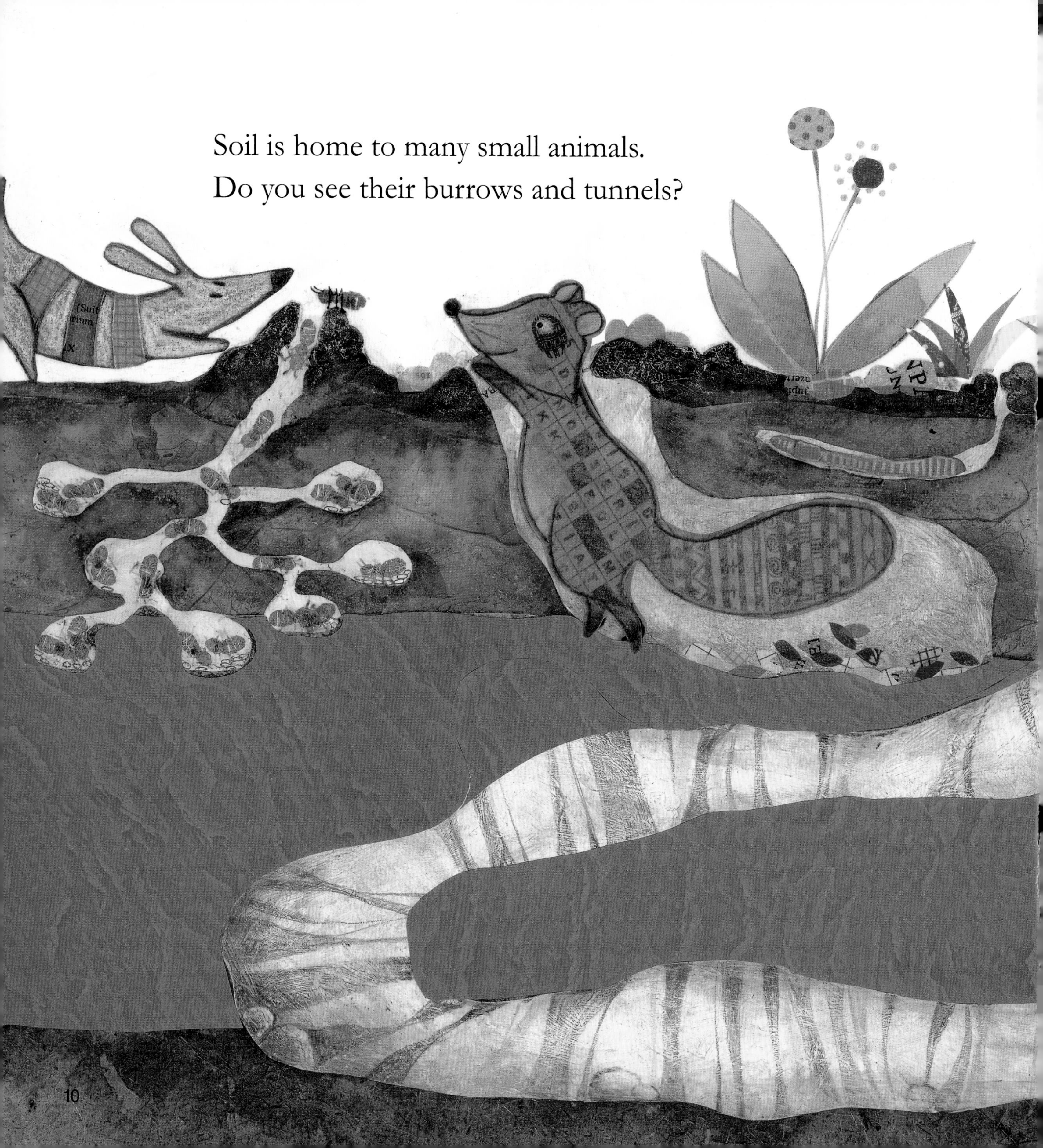

Many kinds of vegetables
and fruits grow in soil.

Apples drop onto the soil.
Leaves flutter down in fall.
What will happen to them?

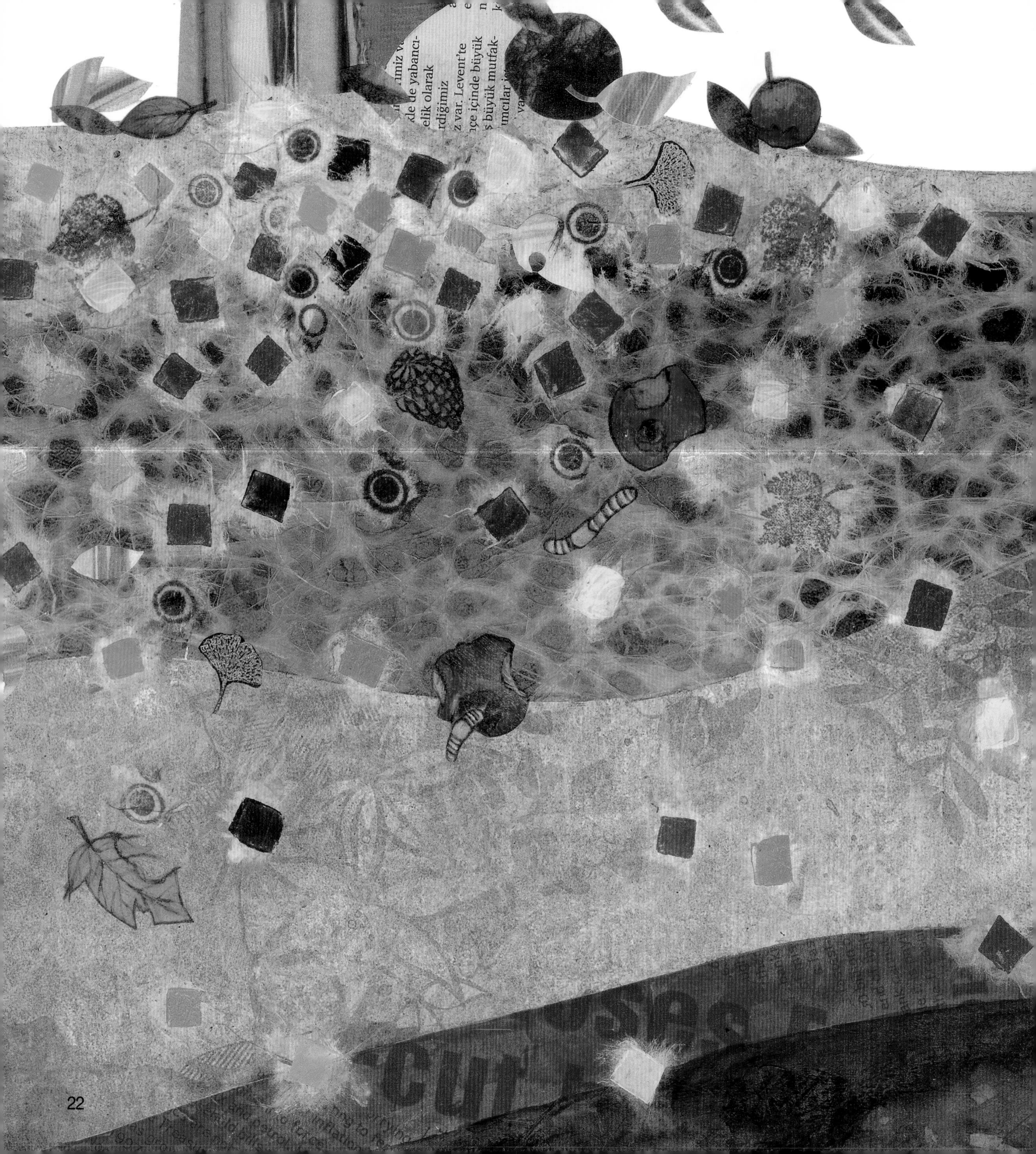

Apples and leaves break down
into small pieces.
They become part of the soil.
When creatures die,
they become soil too.
Soil is made from living things.

Let’s walk on soil with bare feet.
Feel how moist and soft it is.

Soil accepts all of life
and gives to all of life.
It is a living part of our world.

We Can Do Many Things with Soil

Soil helps animals and plants grow. Most of our food comes from plants in the soil. But people use soil in other ways too. Here are some of them.

Dyeing Cloth

Red-colored clay can be used to dye cloth. The cloth's colors become soft orange and yellow. Clay-dyed clothing is a natural way to dye fabric.

Helping Skin

Fine red clay is very soft and contains minerals that are good for our skin. The wet clay is spread over the skin, left until it dries, and then washed off. This is why skin becomes smooth and clean after a facial mud pack.

Making Pottery

Clay hardens when baked at a high temperature. People have made clay pottery for thousands of years. Bowls, cups, floor tiles, and even some toilets are made from clay pottery.

Building Houses

Since ancient times, soil has been used to build houses. It can be used to cover the floor, walls, and ceiling.

What Is in Soil?

Soil contains many things. Let's see the things in soil.

What you need:

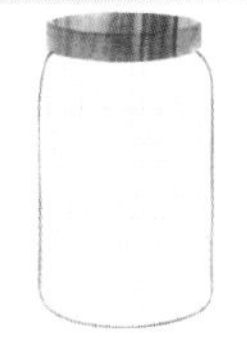

a large clear bottle

soil

water

Instructions:

Fill the clear bottle halfway with soil.

Fill the rest of the bottle with water.

Put the cap on the bottle and shake it to mix the contents.

Do not move the bottle for one or two hours.

Is the soil layered?

After a while, you will see that the soil settles into layers in the bottle. Heavier parts sink to the bottom. Lighter parts stay closer to the top. What do you see in the layers? Do you see small insects and rotten pieces of leaves?

We Need Soil!

Soil covers our planet. It is important to all life. Creatures live and move in soil. Plants grow in soil and use its nutrients. We eat these delicious fruits and vegetables. And both plants and creatures become part of the soil when they die. Soil is important to all life.

Let's think!

Why do animals dig tunnels and burrows in soil?

How do dead creatures and plants break turn into parts of soil?

How do plant roots get nutrients from soil?

What makes soil moist and soft?

Let's do!

Let's see the different parts of soil. Fill a clear bottle halfway with soil. Fill the rest of the bottle with water.
Put the cap on the bottle and shake it to mix the contents.
Leave the bottle for one or two hours.

You will see the soil settles into layers in the bottle.
Heavier parts sink to the bottom.
Lighter parts stay closer to the top.
What do you see in the layers?
Do you see small insects and pieces of leaves?